PUFFIN BOOKS

The Incredible
Shrinking Hippo

The Incredible Shrinking Hippo

Stephanie Baudet

Illustrated by
Debi Gliori

PUFFIN BOOKS

PUFFIN BOOKS

Published by the Penguin Group
Penguin Books Ltd, 80 Strand, London WC2R 0RL, England
Penguin Putnam Inc., 375 Hudson Street, New York, New York 10014, USA
Penguin Books Australia Ltd, 250 Camberwell Road, Camberwell, Victoria 3124, Australia
Penguin Books Canada Ltd, 10 Alcorn Avenue, Toronto, Ontario, Canada M4V 3B2
Penguin Books India (P) Ltd, 11 Community Centre, Panchsheel Park, New Delhi – 110 017, India
Penguin Books (NZ) Ltd, Cnr Rosedale and Airborne Roads, Albany, Auckland, New Zealand
Penguin Books (South Africa) (Pty) Ltd, 24 Sturdee Avenue, Rosebank 2196, South Africa

Penguin Books Ltd, Registered Offices: 80 Strand, London WC2R 0RL, England

www.penguin.com

First published by Hamish Hamilton Ltd 1991
Published in Puffin Books 1995
15 17 19 20 18 16

Text copyright © Stephanie Baudet, 1991
Illustrations copyright © Debi Gliori, 1991
All rights reserved

The moral right of the author and illustrator has been asserted

Printed and bound in China by Leo Paper Products Ltd

0–140–37072–2

It was Sunday when Simon found the
hippopotamus. It looked like a big grey
rock in the middle of the lawn.

"What are you doing here?" he asked.

"Looking for some mud," said the
hippopotamus.

"There's no mud in our garden," said
Simon. "I could put some water in the bath
and you could splash around in that, but
you're too big."

"Oh, that's no problem," said the hippo.

"I can shrink. Just say the word 'tiny'."

"Tiny," said Simon.

The hippo got smaller and smaller until Simon could hold him in the palm of his hand.

"Brilliant!" laughed Simon. "You can be my pet now!"

"I don't want to be a pet!" squeaked the tiny hippo.

"Oh, please!" said Simon. "I'll take you everywhere with me and put you in the bath every day."

"All right, but you must keep me a secret," said Hippo. "I don't like being stared at."

"I promise," said Simon.

"And another thing," said Hippo. "If anyone says the word 'hippopotamus', I'll immediately grow back to my normal size."

Simon nodded, only half listening.

"To make me shrink again," went on Hippo, "you must say any word which means 'tiny', but you can only use the same word once."

"OK," said Simon. He knew several words which meant 'tiny', but he was sure he wouldn't have to use them. "Come on, let's go and play in the bath."

Next day Simon took Hippo to school. He stood Hippo behind the curtain on the classroom window sill.

"What are you doing there, Simon?" shouted Suzie Marks.

"Can I swap seats with you for today, Suzie?" asked Simon.

"No, you can't," she said. "I like sitting by the window." And she lifted her chair down onto the floor with a clatter.

Miss James came in and everyone hurried to their places.

"Good morning, children," she smiled. "Last week we were talking about animals found in Britain. Today we're going to talk about animals found in Africa. The first animal has a funny name which means 'river horse'."

She unrolled a big poster and pinned it to the cork board. "It's a hippopotamus."

Simon gasped and looked towards the curtain. Just behind Suzie's head, the curtain was bulging out and growing fatter and rounder and lumpier.

"Little!" he yelled, making everyone jump.

Miss James looked startled. "Please don't shout out like that, Simon! Hippos certainly aren't little anyway."

The class sniggered. Simon went red. It wasn't easy having a hippo for a pet.

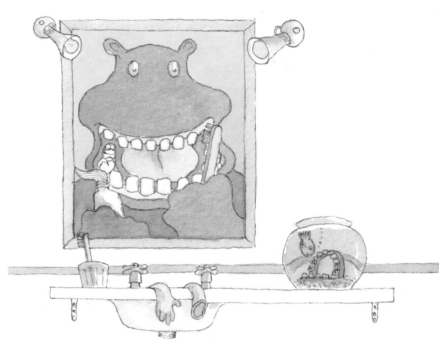

After school Simon's mum took him to the
dentist. He was a nice man with red hair
and a white coat.

"Come and sit here, Simon," he said.
"And let's have a look at your teeth."

Simon climbed onto the chair and lay
back. On the far wall was a big picture. It
was of an animal, grinning widely and
showing two rows of very big teeth.

A hippopotamus!

The dentist looked up. "Lovely teeth they have, hippopotamuses," he said.

Squeak! Creak! Simon's schoolbag began
to burst at the seams.

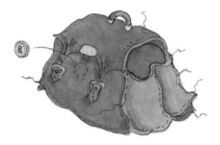

"Schnor!" said Simon, his mouth still
open as the dentist poked at his back teeth.

There was a ripping sound and a small grunt.

"Small!" shouted Simon.

"Yes, that's all," smiled the dentist. "Your teeth are fine – just like our friend the hippo's."

Simon picked up his torn bag and went out. Having a pet hippo did have its problems.

At home Simon went to the bookshelf and took down his dictionary. He turned to the 'T's. There it was. Tiny. He'd said that. And small. And little. There was only a big word left. He sounded it out carefully and hoped he could remember it.

Then he went into the bathroom and put
Hippo in the basin for a wallow.

"Wonderful!" gurgled Hippo, his flabby
top lip slapping the surface of the water. "I
could stay here for hours."

"You can't," said Simon, fishing Hippo
out. "Dad'll be coming in to wash his hands
for dinner soon."

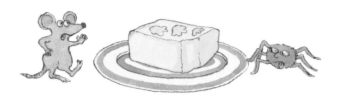

"Not a mouse," said Dad, looking
closely at the butter. "Not a spider either.
These are round footprints – like those of an
elephant or a hippopotamus."

"A hippopotamus!" cried Mum in a loud
voice.

Simon gasped.

A creaking sound came from above.

What was that big word he'd found in the
dictionary?

Then there was a grunt and the ceiling
above cracked under the great weight.

What was that word?

"What's that?" said Dad, jumping up.
"It sounds as if there's an elephant in your
room, Simon."

Then Simon remembered.
"MICROSCOPIC!" he yelled.

The creaking and grunting stopped.
"Just a game," grinned Simon.

Inside he didn't feel like grinning. If that
word was said once more there'd be real
trouble. Hippo had to go. Hippopotamuses
were definitely no good as pets.

But what could he do with a
hippopotamus? Take it to the police
station? Or a pet shop? It was too far to
take it to Africa. The next best thing, he
thought, was the zoo, but there was no
chance of going there soon.

Simon climbed slowly upstairs, thinking hard. He looked out of his window into the street.

A big van stopped next door and two men jumped out. They opened the back doors wide. The van was empty. Simon remembered his mum had said their neighbours were moving today. This must be the van to take their furniture to their new house.

The two men went into the house and Simon stared at the van. It was very tall. It was very wide. A big strong van that could carry a lot of heavy furniture. He smiled, picked up Hippo and ran downstairs and out of the front door.

The men were still inside the house.
Simon walked quietly up to the van. Then
he reached inside as far as he could and
stood Hippo on the floor.

"Goodbye Hippo," he said. "It's been fun
playing with you. These men will take you
to the zoo where there's plenty of mud and
water to wallow in, and you can be your
normal size all the time. I'll come and visit
you when I can."

"Goodbye," said Hippo.

Simon shut the big doors and then ran quickly back to his garden and hid behind the hedge.

The two men came out of the house carrying a piano. Simon watched them struggle with it down the path and into the road. He watched their look of surprise and their cross shouts when they found the van doors closed.

The piano jangled as they put it down in the road. One of the men reached up to open the doors again.

Simon took a deep breath and opened his mouth.

"HIPPOPOTAMUS!" he shouted.

SOS FOR RITA
Hilda Offen

Rita is the youngest in her family and her older
brothers and sister give her the most boring things to do.
What they don't know is that Rita has another identity:
she is also the fabulous Rita the Rescuer!

WHAT STELLA SAW
Wendy Smith

Stella's mum is a fortune teller who always gets things
wrong. But when football-mad Stella starts reading tea-
leaves, she seems to be right every time! Or is she . . .

THE DAY THE SMELLS WENT WRONG
Catherine Sefton

It is just an ordinary day, but Jackie and Phil can't
understand why nothing smells as it should. Toast smells
like tar, fruit smells like fish, and their school dinners
smell of perfume! Together, Jackie and Phil discover the
cause of the problem . . .